Freddy Frogface

For Louis Coplestone,

with

For

Visit Laurence Anholt's website at
www.anholt.co.uk

ORCHARD BOOKS
338 Euston Road
London NW1 3BH
Orchard Books Australia
Level 17/207 Kent Street, Sydney, NSW 2000

First published in Great Britain in 2009

Text © Laurence Anholt 2009
Illustrations © Arthur Robins 2009

The rights of Laurence Anholt to be identified as the author
and of Arthur Robins to be identified as the illustrator
of this work have been asserted by them in accordance
with the Copyright, Designs and Patents Act, 1988.

A CIP catalogue record for this book is available from the British Library.

ISBN 978 1 84616 077 6 (hardback)
ISBN 978 1 84616 315 9 (paperback)

1 2 3 4 5 6 7 8 9 10 (hardback)
1 2 3 4 5 6 7 8 9 10 (paperback)

Printed in China

Orchard Books is a division of Hachette Children's Books,
an Hachette UK company.
www.hachette.co.uk

Seriously SILLY Colour

Laurence Anholt · Arthur Robins

Freddy Frogface

ORCHARD BOOKS

On a log by a bog sat a frog.
His name was Freddy Frogface.

Freddy had a BIG family. Their names were Willy, Jilly, Auntie Sue,

Mummy,
Daddy,
Uncle Hugh,

Granny, Fanny, Cousin Maurice,

Little Bertie
and
Dear Old Doris.

There were also 17 Frogface toddlers and 392 Frogface babies.

Everyone in the bog loved Freddy. He was always making them laugh with silly faces and little tricks and he told such funny jokes . . .

How did the frog feel when he broke his leg?

We don't know, Freddy. How did the frog feel?

UNHOPPY!!

Then everybody croaked with laughter.

CROAK CROAK! THAT'S SUCH A SILLY JOKE!

And even the babies wobbled in their jelly.

Now, not far from the bog
was a grey palace.
It was the home of the Serious
King. He had not laughed
for twenty-seven years.

The Serious King had a beautiful daughter called the Sad Princess.

And the Sad Princess had
a beautiful sausage dog called
the Sad Sausage Dog.

One day the Sad Princess took
the Sad Sausage Dog for a run.
It was very foggy.

She went for a jog in the fog.

She slipped and fell over a log.
She dropped her dog . . .

. . . in
the bog.

Suddenly up popped a frog.

"Please give me my dog,"
said the Princess sadly.
"What will I get in return?"
asked Freddy.
"A great big sloppy kiss,"
said the Sad Princess.

So Freddy pulled the Sad Sausage
Dog out of the bog.

Then he closed his eyes
and waited for the great big
sloppy kiss.

He waited . . .

. . . a long time.

14

When he opened his eyes, the
Sad Princess had jogged away . . .
and so had the sausage dog.

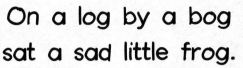

On a log by a bog
sat a sad little frog.

One of the toddler frogs
had an idea. "Let's go to
the Grey Palace and find
Freddy's girlfriend," he said.

So off they went, out of the bog, over the hill and up the steps of the Grey Palace . . .

Willy, Jilly,
    Auntie Sue,
        Mummy, Daddy,
            Uncle Hugh,

Granny, Fanny,
Cousin Maurice,
Little Bertie,
Dear Old Doris,

17 Frogface toddlers
and 392 Frogface babies.

The Frogface family arrived in the
middle of a Serious Dinner Party.
"What funny guests!" said the
Serious King. "If you can make
me smile you may sit next
to my daughter."
So Freddy told a funny joke . . .

How did
the frog lose
his car?

21

Then the Serious King smiled just
a tiny bit.

Freddy hopped up and squeezed
between the Sad Princess and
the Sad Sausage Dog.
He felt very happy.

"Guess what," whispered Freddy.
"If you give me a kiss, I will turn
into a handsome prince."

The Sad Princess gave Freddy
a great big sloppy kiss.

But Freddy did NOT turn into
a handsome prince.

"I forgot," said Freddy.
"You have to kiss my family too!"

So the Sad Princess gave Freddy
another great big sloppy kiss.

She also kissed

Willy, Jilly, Auntie Sue,

Mummy, Daddy, Uncle Hugh,

Granny, Fanny, Cousin Maurice,

Little Bertie and Dear Old Doris.
But still Freddy did not turn into
a handsome prince.

"Don't forget the babies," he said.
So the Sad Princess gave each of
the babies a kiss too.

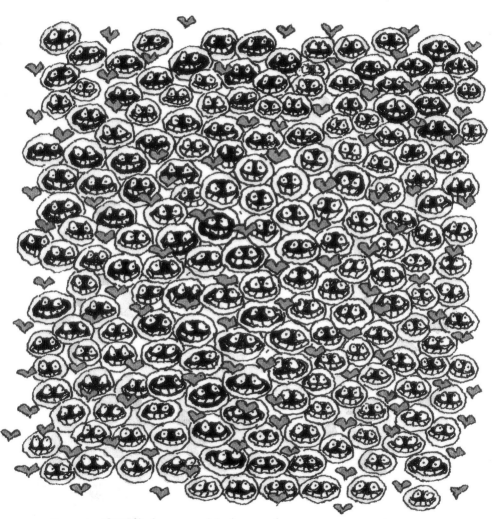

And STILL nothing happened.

It was another one
of Freddy's tricks.

All the little froggies croaked
with laughter.

Then a very funny thing
happened. The Serious King
began to smile . . .

The Serious King began to laugh.
And the Serious King turned into
a Seriously Silly King.

"You may marry my daughter!"
he giggled.
"Oh no!" said Freddy. "I don't
fancy your daughter . . ."

". . . but I love her Sausage Dog."

On a log in the fog by a bog sat a frog and a dog . . .

ENJOY ALL THESE SERIOUSLY SILLY STORIES!

All priced at £4.99

Orchard books are available from all good bookshops, or can be ordered direct from the publisher:
Orchard Books, PO BOX 29, Douglas IM99 1BQ
Credit card orders please telephone: 01624 836000 or fax: 01624 837033
or visit our website: www.orchardbooks.co.uk or e-mail: bookshop@enterprise.net for details.

To order please quote title, author and ISBN and your full name and address.
Cheques and postal orders should be made payable to 'Bookpost plc.'
Postage and packing is FREE within the UK (overseas customers should add £1.00 per book).

Prices and availability are subject to change.